NOUGHTS

& CROSSES

www.malorieblackman.co.uk

NOUGHTS & CROSSES

THE GRAPHIC NOVEL ADAPTATION

malorie
blackman

Adapted by Ian **Edginton**   Illustrated by John **Aggs**

DOUBLEDAY

NOUGHTS & CROSSES : THE GRAPHIC NOVEL ADAPTATION
A DOUBLEDAY BOOK 978 0 857 53195 7

First published in Great Britain by Doubleday,
an imprint of Random House Children's Publishers UK
A Penguin Random House Company

Penguin
Random House
UK

This edition published 2015

1 3 5 7 9 10 8 6 4 2

Original text copyright © Malorie Blackman, 2001, 2015
Text adaptation copyright © Ian Edginton, 2015
Illustrations copyright © John Aggs, 2015

Penguin Random House is committed to a sustainable future for our business, our readers
and our planet. This book is made from Forest Stewardship Council® certified paper.

MIX
Paper from
responsible sources
FSC
www.fsc.org   FSC® C018179

Set in CCComicrazy and CCComicrazy Italic

Random House Children's Publishers UK,
61–63 Uxbridge Road, London W5 5SA

www.randomhousechildrens.co.uk
www.totallyrandombooks.co.uk
www.randomhouse.co.uk

Addresses for companies within The Random House Group Limited
can be found at: www.randomhouse.co.uk/offices.htm

THE RANDOM HOUSE GROUP Limited Reg. No. 954009

A CIP catalogue record for this book is available from the British Library.

Printed in Italy.

For Neil and Lizzy, with love as always. M.B.

For Jane, Constance and Seth.
Who make the future ever brighter. I.E.

UHH...

MRS HADLEY...

LEAVE ME *ALONE!*

WHEN I NEEDED YOUR *HELP,* WHY DIDN'T YOU *GIVE IT?*

I...I THINK I SHOULD GET BACK TO WORK...

YES, YOU *DO THAT!*

'WHERE'VE *YOU* BEEN?'

WELL, WHERE WERE YOU ALL THIS TIME?

HE WAS WITH HIS LITTLE *DAGGER* FRIEND OF COURSE!

HEY! I *WON'T* HEAR THAT LANGUAGE AT THE TABLE!

I WENT FOR A WALK. I WAS THINKING ABOUT SCHOOL... TOMORROW.

MY SON GOING TO *HEATHCROFT*, IMAGINE THAT!

HE DOESN'T NEED TO GO TO *THEIR* SCHOOLS.

WE NOUGHTS SHOULD HAVE OUR *OWN* SCHOOLS WITH THE SAME OPPORTUNITIES AS THE CROSSES!

WE DON'T NEED TO MIX WITH THEM!

AS LONG AS THE SCHOOLS ARE RUN BY CROSSES, WE'LL ALWAYS BE TREATED AS SECOND-CLASS... SECOND *BEST*.

WE SHOULD LOOK AFTER OUR *OWN* AND NOT WAIT FOR THEM TO DO IT FOR US.

YOU NEVER *USED* TO BELIEVE THAT.

YES, WELL... I'M NOT AS *NAÏVE* AS I WAS.

IT'LL BE FINE MUM, DON'T WORRY.

YEAH, WELL DON'T GO GETTING TOO BIG FOR YOUR BOOTS.

YOU'LL SOON BE THINKING YOU'RE TOO *GOOD* FOR US!

OF COURSE HE *WON'T.* YOU'LL BE REPRESENTING ALL OF US NOUGHTS AT THE SCHOOL.

YOU MUST SHOW THEM THEY'RE *WRONG* ABOUT US.

SHOW THEM WE'RE *JUST* AS GOOD AS *THEY* ARE.

HE DOESN'T NEED TO GO TO THAT STUCK UP SCHOOL TO SHOW THEM THAT!

MEG, IF OUR BOY'S GOING TO GET *ANYWHERE* IN THIS LIFE, HE HAS TO LEARN TO PLAY THE GAME BY *THEIR* RULES.

HE JUST HAS TO BE *BETTER* AT IT, THAT'S ALL.

DON'T YOU WANT SOMETHING *MORE* FOR YOUR SON THAN *WE* EVER HAD?

THOSE BLEEDING HEART *LIBERALS* IN THE PANGAEAN ECONOMIC COMMUNITY MAKE ME *SICK!*

THEY SAID WE HAD TO OPEN OUR SCHOOLS TO NOUGHTS, SO WE *DID.*

THAT WE OUGHT TO RECRUIT NOUGHTS INTO THE POLICE AND ARMED FORCES, SO WE *DID.*

AND THEY'RE *STILL* NOT SATISFIED!

AND AS FOR THE LIBERATION MILITIA! I THOUGHT LETTING A FEW *BLANKERS* INTO OUR SCHOOLS WOULD SHUT THEM UP!

IT WASN'T ENOUGH. THEY HAD THEIR DEMANDS MET, SO THEY DON'T SEE WHY THEY CAN'T HAVE A FEW MORE AND THERE'LL BE MORE AFTER THAT.

OVER MY DEAD *BODY!*

'SO, WHERE HAVE *YOU* BEEN UNTIL TEN O'CLOCK AT NIGHT?'

WELL?

I WAS WALKING. I HAD A LOT TO THINK ABOUT.

ARE YOU *OK*, SON? I WENT DOWN TO THE SCHOOL BUT THE POLICE WOULDN'T LET ME IN.

THEY SAID I'D NO OFFICIAL BUSINESS ON THE PREMISES.

I WAS OK. ONCE WE GOT INTO SCHOOL, IT WAS ALL RIGHT.

WELL, YOU'RE IN THERE NOW CALLUM. DON'T LET ANY DAGGER SWINE DRIVE YOU OUT – *UNDERSTAND?*

EXCUSE ME, *LANGUAGE!*

SORRY, LOVE.

'I'LL TELL HIM THE TRUTH.'

HI, MIND IF I JOIN YOU?

WHAT'RE YOU *DOING*?

EATING MY LUNCH!

HI, I'M SEPHY HADLEY!

UHM, I'M SHANIA.

HOW'S YOUR HEAD?

IT'S OK. THANKS FOR ASKING.

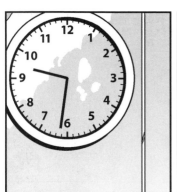

WALK! NO RUNNING! *WALK!*

SEPHY... *WAIT.*

HOW ARE YOU? ARE YOU OK?

YES, THANK YOU.

I'M GLAD.

OH, MY GIRL.

WHERE'S JED, DADDY?

HE'S GONE LOVE. HIS FAMILY MOVED AWAY A LONG TIME AGO.

NO...NOT LONG AGO... YESTERDAY...LAST WEEK.

I'M...I'M SEVENTEEN.

SWEETHEART, YOU'RE TWENTY. TWENTY LAST APRIL.

I THOUGHT I WAS SEVENTEEN... EIGHTEEN. I...I DON'T KNOW WHAT I THOUGHT.

LYNNY, I'M SORRY. I DIDN'T KNOW.

KEEP YOUR HANDS OFF ME!

MY NOUGHT HANDS YOU MEAN.

ANYONE IN THIS ROOM CAN BE A SCIENTIST OR AN ASTRONAUT OR ANYTHING YOU WANT TO BE IF YOU WORK HARD AND ARE DETERMINED.

RIGHT THEN, WHO KNOWS WHO INVENTED AUTOMATIC TRAFFIC SIGNALS WHICH LED TO THE TRAFFIC LIGHTS WE USE TODAY?

HE ALSO INVENTED A TYPE OF GAS MASK USED DURING WORLD WAR ONE?

ANYONE?

YES CALLUM?

GARRET MORGAN, SIR.

CORRECT. WHAT ABOUT THIS ONE.

WHO PIONEERED BLOOD BANKS?

COME ON. ANYONE?

YES, CALLUM? ENLIGHTEN US.

DR. CHARLES DREW.

NOT IN *MY* SCHOOL THEY WON'T! IF THE BLANKERS ARE FINDING IT TOUGH, PERHAPS THEY SHOULD GO ELSEWHERE!

NO ONE *WANTED* THEM HERE IN THE *FIRST* PLACE!

I DID. SO DID SOME OF THE OTHER TEACHERS *AND* THE GOVERNMENT AND...

THE GOVERNMENT DID AS THE PANGAEAN ECONOMIC COMMUNITY ORDERED! THEY WERE AFRAID OF SANCTIONS, THAT'S WHY.

THE *REASON* DOESN'T MATTER. THE POINT IS, THEY *DID* IT. THE NOUGHTS ARE HERE AND IT'S UP TO US MAKE THIS SCHOOL A *SANCTUARY,* A HAVEN FOR CROSSES *AND* NOUGHTS.

ONE WHERE WE PROVIDE **EQUALITY** OF EDUCATION, OF OPPORTUNITY AND TREATMENT.

AND IF WE DON'T ACT SOON, THIS WHOLE SCHEME WILL *FAIL.* OR IS THAT THE *POINT?*

MRS PAXTON, ARE YOU *REALLY* THAT *NAÏVE?* NOUGHTS ARE TREATED THE SAME HERE AS THEY WOULD BE OUTSIDE...

AND *THAT'S* THE PROBLEM!

ENOUGH! *ENOUGH!*

DON'T YOU HAVE A CLASS SOON?

MR JASON DIDN'T LIKE IT WHEN I SAID NOUGHTS HAD DONE THINGS TOO. HE DOESN'T LIKE ANYTHING I SAY OR DO.

HE JUST DOESN'T WANT TO SEE YOU FAIL. BEING HARD ON YOU IS HIS WAY OF TRYING TO...

TO WHAT?

CALLUM, A CHANGE OF POLICY WAS LONG OVERDUE AT THIS SCHOOL...AT ALL THE SCHOOLS.

BELIEVE ME, MR JASON DOESN'T WANT TO SEE YOU FAIL ANY MORE THAN I DO.

HE TOLD YOU THIS, DID HE?

HE DIDN'T HAVE TO.

YEAH, RIGHT.

CALLUM, I'M GOING TO TELL YOU SOMETHING IN THE STRICTEST CONFIDENCE. I'M GOING TO TRUST YOU. OK?

OK...

MR JASON ISN'T AGAINST YOU...

BECAUSE HIS OWN MOTHER WAS A NOUGHT.

Later.

DON'T TREAT ME LIKE THIS KAMAL, I WON'T *STAND* FOR IT.

THEN GO AND HAVE ANOTHER DRINK OR EIGHT! THAT'S ABOUT *ALL* YOU'RE *GOOD* FOR THESE DAYS!

YOU'RE A *CRUEL* MAN!

KAMAL, WHAT'VE I DONE TO *DESERVE* THIS? I'VE *ALWAYS* BEEN A GOOD WIFE TO YOU. A GOOD *MOTHER* TO OUR CHILDREN.

AND *YOU'RE* A *DRUNK!* WORSE THAN THAT, YOU'RE A BORING *DRUNK!*

OH, YES. YOU'VE BEEN AN EXCELLENT MOTHER TO *ALL* MY CHILDREN!

I *SHOULD* HAVE LET YOU BRING YOUR SON INTO OUR HOUSE. I KNOW THAT NOW. BUT WHEN YOU TOLD ME, I WAS HURT. I MADE A *MISTAKE*.

SO DID *I*, WHEN I *MARRIED* YOU!

YOU WANTED TO PUNISH ME FOR MY SON WHO WAS BORN BEFORE WE EVER *MET!*

THE GREAT JASMINE ADEYEBE-HADLEY BRINGING UP HER HUSBAND'S CHILD AS HER *OWN?* THAT'D *NEVER* DO!

GOD *FORBID*, YOU MIGHT CHIP A *NAIL* OR DIRTY ONE OF YOUR DESIGNER GOWNS!

THEN, I...I'LL *DIVORCE* YOU! I'LL TELL THE *NEWSPAPERS!*

JASMINE, THE DAY YOU DIVORCE ME WILL BE THE HAPPIEST DAY OF MY LIFE.

MINNIE...

WHAT D'YOU WANT FROG FACE?

I THINK MOTHER AND DAD ARE GETTING A DIVORCE.

WON'T HAPPEN. HE'S BEEN THREATENING HER WITH THAT FOR YEARS.

BUT SHE THREATENED *HIM* THIS TIME. AND WHAT ABOUT OUR BROTHER? AREN'T YOU *CURIOUS?*

HE'S NOT OUR BROTHER, HE'S JUST DAD'S SON. BESIDES, I WASN'T CURIOUS ABOUT HIM *THREE YEARS* AGO, WHY START NOW.

THREE YEARS! WHY DIDN'T YOU *TELL* ME?

WHAT'S TO TELL? DAD HAD A FLING BEFORE HE MET MOTHER AND HAD A SON.

I THINK SHE ONLY HAD HER AFFAIR TO MAKE DAD SIT UP AND TAKE NOTICE. BUT IF ANYTHING IT DROVE THEM FURTHER APART.

SHE HAD AN *AFFAIR?*

I THINK... SHE WAS LONELY.

BUT SHE'S GOT *LOADS* OF FRIENDS.

NOT CLOSE ONES. NOT *REAL* ONES.

SHE'S PROBABLY DRIVEN THEM ALL AWAY WITH HER FUNNY MOODS.

ONE MINUTE SHE'S PUSHING ME AWAY, ACTING AS IF I DON'T EXIST.

NEXT SHE WANTS TO KNOW ABOUT EVERY MINUTE OF MY DAY.

WHY DOESN'T SHE MAKE SOME NEW FRIENDS THEN?

YOU'RE VERY YOUNG SEPHY.

DON'T BE *PATRONISING!*

I'M NOT, I'M JUST STATING A FACT, AND YOU KNOW WHAT I WISH FOR YOU?

WHAT?

THAT YOU NEVER GROW OLDER.

Meanwhile.

MINERVA, WHAT IF...

AH, THERE YOU ARE. IT'S A SHAME YOU TWO DIDN'T HAVE YOUR WITS ABOUT YOU.

IT'S CLEAR WHICH SIDE OF THE FAMILY YOU TAKE AFTER.

SHSHH. IT'LL BE ALL RIGHT. MOTHER WILL BE FINE. YOU'LL SEE...SHE'LL BE FINE.

EXCUSE ME?

YOU SHOULD'VE PHONED ME FIRST INSTEAD OF AN AMBULANCE, AND ON A LAND LINE OF ALL THINGS!

THE STORY'S ALREADY OUT THAT SHE TOOK AN OVERDOSE BECAUSE YOUR FATHER'S FOUND SOMEONE ELSE.

MOTHER TRIED TO COMMIT SUICIDE!

AN AMBULANCE WAS MORE IMPORTANT THAN CALLING FATHER'S SECRETARY, MISS AYELETTE!

THAT'S PERSONAL SECRETARY, MISS HADLEY—AND FOR YOUR INFORMATION, ANYONE WHO REALLY WANTS TO KILL THEMSELVES TAKES MORE THAN FOUR SLEEPING TABLETS.

SHE JUST DID IT FOR THE ATTENTION AND SYMPATHY.

HI, SANCHEZ? LISTEN. WE NEED TO CALL IN A FEW FAVOURS. I'M AT THE HOSPITAL AND

...YES, OF COURSE SHE'S FINE...IT'S NOTHING AT ALL, I PROMISE YOU BUT WE NEED TO SPREAD THE WORD THAT IT WAS AN ACCIDENT, NOTHING MORE...

WHU...

YOU-

YOU CAN GO TO *HELL!*

YOU...

WHAT? WHAT AM I MISS PERSONAL SECRETARY?

YOU'RE A SPOILT *BRAT!*

AND *YOU'RE* AN INSENSITIVE *COW!*

THAT WAS ELECTRIC, MINERVA! *ELECTRIC!*

One Week Later.

'SUCH A TRAGEDY...'

'I'M SO SORRY...'

'BEAUTIFUL GIRL...'

'IF YOU NEED ANYTHING...'

NONSENSE. YOU'VE COME THIS FAR. SHE CAN'T LEAVE WITHOUT A DRINK, CAN SHE RYAN?

HELLO MISS HADLEY.

I...I'LL GO.

SEPHY, WAIT...

YEAH, *GO!* GO ON! WHO TOLD YOU TO COME HERE IN THE *FIRST PLACE?*

WHERE WAS *SHE* THE LAST *THREE YEARS* WHEN LYNNY WAS OUT OF HER HEAD AND WE DIDN'T HAVE *TWO BEANS* TO RUB TOGETHER?

JUDE, THAT'S *ENOUGH.*

NO, IT'S *NOT.* HE'S RIGHT.

WHERE WAS THIS *DAGGER* WHEN YOU GOT *FIRED* MUM, AND *I* HAD TO DROP OUT OF SCHOOL?

WHERE WAS *SHE* WHEN HARRY OVER THERE GOT THE BOOT?

BUT... THEY TOLD ME YOU'D QUIT.

QUIT? I GOT *FIRED* AFTER THAT RIOT AT YOUR SCHOOL!

WHEN YOUR FACE WAS PLASTERED ALL OVER THE TELLY AND I WAS NOWHERE TO BE SEEN, YOUR MOTHER KICKED ME OUT SO FAST I'LL HAVE HER BOOT PRINT ON MY BACKSIDE 'TIL THE DAY I DIE!

I...DIDN'T *KNOW.* I *SWEAR.*

DIDN'T TAKE THE TROUBLE TO *FIND OUT* EITHER I'LL BET?

YOU AND *YOUR KIND* HAVE BROUGHT US NOTHING BUT *GRIEF!*

PERSEPHONE, I THINK IT'S BEST YOU LEFT.

BUT, I HAVEN'T DONE ANYTHING...

THAT'S RIGHT, YOU HAVEN'T. YOU COME HERE IN YOUR FANCY DRESS WHICH COSTS MORE THAN I MAKE IN A YEAR AND WE'RE SUPPOSED TO SMILE AND BE GRATEFUL. IS THAT *IT?*

NO...

GO ON, *GET LOST* BEFORE I DO SOMETHING I'LL REGRET!

YOU HAD NO RIGHT TO DO THAT!

YES HE DID. SHE WASN'T *WANTED* HERE. HE ONLY TOLD HER THE **TRUTH.**

RYAN...?

ENOUGH'S ENOUGH, MEGGIE. IT'S TIME FOR A CHANGE. MY INEFFECTUAL AND USELESS DAYS ARE *OVER!*

I'M *SORRY* SWEETHEART, I'M A BIT ON EDGE. IF *YOU* DON'T HELP ME, NO ONE ELSE WILL.

Y-YOUR FATHER HASN'T EVEN BEEN TO SEE ME. NOT A *PHONE CALL* OR A CARD.

MY TWO BEST GIRLS. HERE'S A LITTLE LIFE LESSON FOR YOU.

NEVER MAKE A *MISTAKE*,

BECAUSE IT WILL NEVER BE *FORGIVEN* OR FORGOTTEN.

I MADE A MISTAKE ONCE. I DID SOMETHING I SHOULDN'T HAVE. BUT... I WAS *LONELY*.

YOUR FATHER WAS NEVER AT HOME AND I WAS SO *TIRED* OF BEING *ALONE*.

BUT HE FOUND OUT. I MADE A MISTAKE AND I'VE NEVER STOPPED PAYING FOR IT.

SO DON'T BE LIKE ME. BE *PERFECT*.

BE MY PERFECT LITTLE GIRLS.

Six months later.

BREEPBREEP-BREEPBREEP-CLICK

BREEPBREEP-BREEPBREEP-CLICK

CALLUM?

SEPHY? I'M GLAD YOU REMEMBERED OUR RING CODE.

I THOUGHT IT WAS GOING TO BE YOUR MUM.

SHE *STILL* WON'T LET ME HAVE MY OWN PHONE.

WE'RE ABOUT TO GO OUT, TO DO SOME SHOPPING, NEW SCHOOL CLOTHES AND SHOES.

POOR YOU. SPENDING ALL THAT LOVELY MONEY.

IT'S NOT *FUNNY.* SHE'S BEEN FULL ON ALL THE TIME SINCE SHE LEFT HOSPITAL.

AT LEAST WHEN WE'RE OUT SHE'S NOT *DRINKING... MOSTLY.*

I...I'D *MUCH* RATHER BE WITH YOU.

CALLUM?

I'M STILL HERE.

HOW ABOUT I MEET YOU THERE? DUNDALE SHOPPING CENTRE, RIGHT?

'JUST UNDER THIRTY MINUTES AGO, A BOMB EXPLODED AT THE WORLD FAMOUS DUNDALE SHOPPING CENTRE, KILLING AT LEAST SEVEN AND SERIOUSLY INJURING DOZENS MORE.'

CASUALTIES ARE BEING TAKEN BY GROUND AND AIR AMBULANCE TO LOCAL HOSPITALS. ALL HOSPITALS IN THE AREA ARE ON FULL ALERT.

OH *NO!* PLEASE...NO.

MUM! DAD!

CALLUM! THANK *GOD!* YOU'RE ALL RIGHT!

SSH! LISTEN.

A WARNING WAS ISSUED BY THE NOUGHT GROUP CALLING ITSELF THE LIBERATION MILITIA ONLY FIVE MINUTES BEFORE THE EXPLOSION.

A SENIOR POLICE OFFICER ON THE SCENE BELIEVES THE BOMB WAS PLANTED IN A CAFÉ BIN INSIDE THE SHOPPING CENTRE BUT STATED IT WAS TOO EARLY TO SPECULATE.

THAT'S A *LIE!*

HOW WOULD *YOU* KNOW?

THAT'S *ENOUGH,* JUDE!

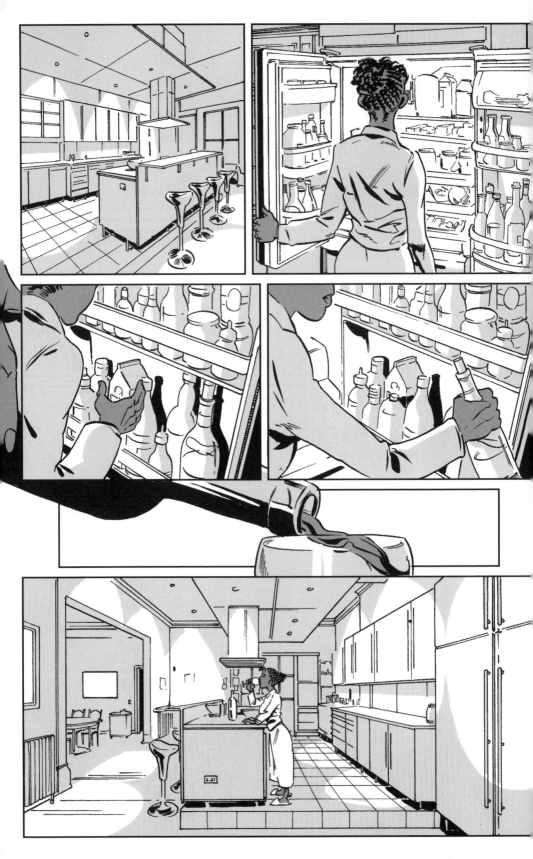

SEPHY, *PROMISE* ME YOU WON'T DRINK ANY MORE.

NO...BUT I PROMISE I'LL **TRY.**

WHU—

DON'T YOU WANT TO SEE WHAT KISSING'S LIKE ANY MORE – *HUH?*

YOU... YOU STINK OF BOOZE.

Y'KNOW CALLUM. SOMETIMES YOU CAN BE JUST AS *CRUEL* AS MY DAD IS TO MY MOTHER.

SEPHY! SEPHY, I'M SORRY.

GET LOST!

NOT WITHOUT YOU.

PIN

'I WANT...I *NEED* TO GET AWAY FROM HERE, FROM EVERYTHING.'

COME *ON!* WE KNOW ALL *ABOUT* YOUR FAMILY'S INVOLVEMENT!

WHAT D'YOU NEED *ME* FOR THEN?

CORROBORATION. CONFIRM WHAT WE KNOW ALREADY AND WE'LL GO EASY ON YOU.

HOW MANY *TIMES?* I'VE ALREADY TOLD YOU, I DON'T KNOW *ANYTHING!*

DON'T MESS US ABOUT, SON.

I'M NOT YOUR SON!

AND *I'M* NOT SOMEONE YOU WANT TO MAKE AN *ENEMY* OF!

WHOSE IDEA WAS THE DUNDALE BOMB? YOUR *BROTHER'S* OR YOUR OLD MAN'S?

YOU *HATE* ALL CROSSES, *DON'T* YOU!

YOU'D DO WHATEVER IT TOOK TO *WIPE OUT* THE LOT OF US. ISN'T THAT *RIGHT?*

PLEASE, NO MORE QUESTIONS... I'M SO TIRED...

PLEASE...

CALLUM?

MUM?

ARE YOU OK? THEY DIDN'T HURT YOU?

W-WHERE'S DAD? WHERE'S JUDE?

YOUR DAD'S STILL BEING QUESTIONED. I DON'T KNOW WHERE JUDE IS. HE DIDN'T COME HOME LAST NIGHT.

THEY FOUND AN EMPTY DRINKS CAN NEAR TO WHERE THE BOMB WENT OFF. THEY SAID IT HAD JUDE'S PRINTS ALL OVER IT.

HOW DO THEY KNOW *THAT?*

FROM THE PRINT ON HIS ID CARD, WHEN IT WAS SCANNED AT THE HOSPITAL.

I GUESS THEY TOOK IT FROM THE COMPUTER BEFORE THE NURSE DELETED IT – IF SHE EVER *DID.*

BUT JUDE DIDN'T...*DID* HE?

THEY'RE SAYING HE PLANTED THE BOMB. THEY'RE SAYING HE...HE'LL HANG FOR IT.

THEY'VE ISSUED A REWARD FOR INFORMATION LEADING TO HIS CAPTURE. *FIFTY THOUSAND.*

IF THEY ONLY WANT JUDE, WHY'RE THEY STILL QUESTIONING DAD?

I'VE NO IDEA. HE DEMANDED TO SEE THEM ONCE HE KNEW WHY THEY WERE AFTER JUDE.

YOU TWO CAN GO.

WHERE'S MY *HUSBAND?*

HE'S BEING HELD, AFTER WHICH HE'LL BE FORMALLY CHARGED.

CHARGED WITH *WHAT?*

MY HUSBAND'S DONE NOTHING WRONG. WHY'S HE BEING HELD?

GET YOUR THINGS AND LEAVE. I HAVEN'T GOT ALL DAY!

I *DEMAND* TO KNOW WHY YOU'RE HOLDING MY HUSBAND! I WANT TO SEE HIM – *NOW!*

YOU CAN *LEAVE* OR SPEND THE REST OF THE NIGHT IN THIS CELL. IT'S YOUR CHOICE.

NO ONE BUT HIS LAWYER CAN SEE HIM UNTIL AFTER HE'S FORMALLY CHARGED.

CHARGED WITH WHAT?

POLITICAL TERRORISM AND *SEVEN* COUNTS OF *MURDER.*

RYAN...

NO, LOVE. I'M *GUILTY*. THAT'S THE TRUTH AND I'M STICKING TO IT. I WON'T LET THEM PUT YOU OR CALLUM AWAY FOR THIS. *OR JUDE.*

JUST MAKE SURE JUDE STAYS LOST SO THE DAGGERS CAN'T GET THEIR HANDS ON HIM.

IF THEY FIND HIM, HE'LL ROT IN PRISON BUT AT LEAST MY CONFESSION MEANS HE WON'T DIE.

Later.

'TODAY, RYAN CALLUM McGREGOR WAS FORMALLY CHARGED WITH POLITICAL TERRORISM AND SEVEN COUNTS OF MURDER FOR THE BOMBING OF THE DUNDALE SHOPPING CENTRE.'

HE HAS CONFESSED TO ALL CHARGES.

HIS FAMILY, CONSISTING OF HIS WIFE MARGARET AND SONS, JUDE AND CALLUM, ARE SAID TO BE IN HIDING.

BREAKING NEWS

BLANKER *SCUMBAG!*

HIS WHOLE FAMILY SHOULD SWING!

MINERVA! I WON'T HAVE SUCH LANGUAGE IN THIS HOUSE.

YES, *MOTHER.* TO THINK. WE HAD HIM **HERE,** IN *THIS* HOUSE.

AND HIS WIFE ACTUALLY USED TO WORK HERE. IF THE PRESS HEAR OF IT, THEY'LL HAVE A FIELD DAY — DAD WILL HAVE *KITTENS!*

WHAT D'YOU MEAN?

USE YOUR BRAIN! IF RYAN MCGREGOR GETS OFF, DAD WILL BE ACCUSED OF **FAVOURITISM** WHETHER OR NOT IT HAS ANYTHING TO DO WITH HIM.

MOTHER, THEY WON'T REALLY HANG MR MCGREGOR WILL THEY?

IF HE'S GUILTY...

AND *CALLUM* GOES TO OUR SCHOOL. DAD'S GOING TO GET IT IN THE NECK FOR THAT TOO!

CALLUM'S GOT *NOTHING* TO DO WITH THIS!

AN APPLE NEVER FALLS FAR FROM THE TREE!

EVEN IF RYAN MCGREGOR *IS* GUILTY— WHICH I DON'T BELIEVE FOR ONE SECOND –

THAT DOESN'T MEAN CALLUM –

OH, PERSEPHONE. *GROW UP!*

IT'S ALL UP IN THE AIR. NOTHING'S BEEN DECIDED YET.

'CALLUM, THERE'S NO EASY WAY TO SAY THIS, SO I'M GOING TO GET RIGHT TO THE POINT.'

UNTIL THE MATTER WITH YOUR FATHER IS RESOLVED,

THE GOVERNORS AND I HAVE DECIDED IT WOULD SERVE EVERYONE'S BEST INTERESTS IF YOU WERE *SUSPENDED* FOR A WHILE.

I'M GUILTY UNTIL MY DAD'S PROVEN *INNOCENT?* IS THAT HOW IT WORKS?

YOU MUST BE *SO* THRILLED. THREE DOWN, ONLY *ONE* MORE TO GO!

COLIN'S GONE AND YOU COULDN'T *WAIT* TO GET RID OF SHANIA AND NOW IT'S *MY* TURN!

SHANIA WAS EXPELLED FOR GROSS MISCONDUCT.

SHE SLAPPED GARDNER WILSON AFTER HE *HIT* HER! EVERYONE KNOWS IT, EVEN *YOU*.

WHY ISN'T IT GROSS MISCONDUCT WHEN A *CROSS* DOES IT?

I HAVE NO INTENTION OF JUSTIFYING SCHOOL POLICY TO YOU. WE'LL REVIEW YOUR *SITUATION* ONCE THE DUST HAS SETTLED.

GOOD LUCK TO YOU CALLUM.

YEAH, *RIGHT.*

CALLUM! CALLUM, COME HERE AT *ONCE.*

I SAID COME *BACK* HERE!

MINNIE?

MINNIE

GO AWAY!

DON'T YOUR *EARS* WORK?

JUST HEAR ME OUT.

I...I WANT TO ASK YOUR ADVICE ABOUT SOMETHING.

OH, YES?

WHAT WOULD YOU SAY IF I TOLD YOU I'M THINKING OF GOING AWAY TO BOARDING SCHOOL? TO CHIVERS.

I THINK IT'S AN *EXCELLENT* IDEA. WHICH IS WHY I ASKED MOTHER THE *SAME* THING A FEW WEEKS AGO.

YOU *DID?*

YOU'RE NOT THE ONLY ONE WHO NEEDS TO GET OUT OF HERE.

IS IT THAT *OBVIOUS?*

SEPHY, YOU AND I HAVE NEVER GOT ON, AND I'M SORRY ABOUT THAT.

MAYBE IF WE'D BEEN ABLE TO COUNT ON EACH OTHER WE'D HAVE DONE BETTER.

The Trial

RYAN CALLUM MCGREGOR. YOU HAVE HEARD THE CHARGES READ TO YOU. ON THE CHARGE OF POLITICAL TERRORISM HOW DO YOU PLEAD?

GUILTY OR NOT GUILTY?

DAD, DON'T DO IT!

ANY MORE OUTBURSTS FROM THE PUBLIC GALLERY AND I WILL HAVE THE MEMBERS OF THE PUBLIC EVICTED FROM THIS COURT!

I HOPE I'VE MADE MYSELF UNDERSTOOD!

The trial.

DO YOU SWEAR TO TELL THE TRUTH, THE WHOLE TRUTH AND NOTHING BUT THE TRUTH?

I DO.

COULD YOU STATE YOUR **FULL NAME** FOR THE RECORD, PLEASE?

CALLUM RYAN MCGREGOR.

AND DO YOU BELONG TO THE **LIBERATION MILITIA**?

OBJECTION! CALLUM MCGREGOR IS **NOT** ON TRIAL HERE.

IT GOES TO WITNESS CREDIBILITY, YOUR HONOUR.

I'LL ALLOW IT.

CALLUM, DO YOU BELONG—

NO, I DON'T!

WHAT ABOUT YOUR FATHER?

HE DOESN'T *EITHER.* MY FATHER WOULDN'T HURT A *FLY!*

WHEREAS THE LIBERATION MILITIA *WOULD?*

WHAT'S YOUR OPINION OF THE L.M?

OBJECTION!

OVERRULED!

ANY ORGANIZATION WHICH PROMOTES EQUALITY BETWEEN NOUGHTS AND CROSSES IS...

YES?

NOUGHTS AND CROSSES SHOULD BE EQUAL. I SUPPORT ANYONE WHO TRIES TO BRING THAT ABOUT.

AND THE END JUSTIFIES THE MEANS DOES IT?

YOUR HONOUR—

WITHDRAWN.

SO NO ONE IN YOUR FAMILY KNEW ANYTHING ABOUT THE DUNDALE BOMBING?

THAT'S CORRECT.

INCLUDING YOU?

INCLUDING ME.

YOUR HONOUR, I CALL INTO EVIDENCE EXHIBIT D19.

YOUR HONOUR, THIS SECURITY CAMERA FOOTAGE FROM THE DUNDALE SHOPPING CENTRE HAS BEEN COMPILED BY THE POLICE, MY OFFICE AND TWO PROMINENT INDEPENDENT WITNESSES FROM THE NOUGHT COMMUNITY.

YOUR HONOUR, I *STRENUOUSLY* OBJECT! I HAVEN'T HAD CHANCE TO VIEW THESE TAPES—

I ONLY ACQUIRED THEM YESTERDAY EVENING AND MY COLLEAGUES HAVE WORKED THROUGH THE NIGHT TO ASSEMBLE THIS FOOTAGE—

YOUR HONOUR, I MUST *INSIST* ON BEING ALLOWED TO VIEW THEM BEFORE THEY'RE ENTERED INTO EVIDENCE –

YOUR HONOUR, THERE ARE PRECEDENTS FOR PRESENTING EVIDENCE NOT SEEN BY THE DEFENCE –

I AM AWARE OF THAT MR PINGULE. YOU'RE NOT THE *ONLY* ONE WHO WENT TO LAW SCHOOL.

I WILL ALLOW IT.

CALLUM, CAN YOU TELL ME WHAT YOU WERE DOING AT THE DUNDALE, TEN MINUTES BEFORE THE BOMB WENT OFF?

I CAN'T REMEMBER.

LET'S SEE IF I CAN *REFRESH* YOUR MEMORY.

IN THIS FILM, WHO ARE YOU PULLING FROM THE CUCKOO'S EGG CAFÉ?

SEPHY...

PERSEPHONE HADLEY? KAMAL HADLEY'S DAUGHTER?

YES. SHE'S A FRIEND.

WHY WERE YOU IN SUCH A *HURRY* TO GET HER OUT OF THERE?

I SAID I'D MEET HER, I WAS *LATE*. I WAS AFRAID HER MUM WOULD APPEAR AT ANY SECOND... I WANTED TO SHOW HER SOMETHING.

WHAT, EXACTLY?

I DON'T REMEMBER. WITH EVERYTHING THAT'S HAPPENED...

IT WAS SOMETHING SILLY — A CAR OR PLANE OR SOMETHING.

INDEED. NO FURTHER QUESTIONS.

YOU MAY STEP DOWN.

JUST A MOMENT CALLUM. COULD YOU DESCRIBE YOUR RELATIONSHIP WITH **MRS HADLEY**, PERSEPHONE'S MOTHER?

SHE DOESN'T LIKE ME. SHE TOLD HER SECRETARY NOT TO LET ME INTO HER HOUSE.

SEPHY... *PERSEPHONE* WAS BEATEN UP AT SCHOOL. MRS HADLEY BLAMED ME.

WHY? DID *YOU* DO IT?

NO, OF *COURSE* NOT! SOME GIRLS FROM THE YEAR ABOVE HER DID!

YOUR HONOUR, IS THERE A *POINT* TO THIS?

I'M *JUST* COMING TO IT.

CALLUM, IF MRS HADLEY HAD BEEN THERE *TOO* WHAT WOULD YOU HAVE DONE?

I WANTED TO SHOW SEPHY SOMETHING BUT IT WOULDN'T HAVE BEEN THE END OF THE WORLD IF I HADN'T.

I WOULD'VE WAITED UNTIL SHE WAS ALONE. I WASN'T IN A HURRY.

THANK YOU CALLUM. THAT WILL BE ALL.

Later.

MISS HADLEY, DID CALLUM GIVE YOU A *REASON* WHY YOU SHOULD LEAVE THE CAFÉ?

HE WANTED TO SHOW ME SOMETHING OUTSIDE.

I DON'T KNOW WHAT. IT WAS GOING TO BE A **SURPRISE** BUT THE BOMB WENT OFF BEFORE HE COULD TELL ME.

AND THAT'S THE *TRUTH?*

YES.

I KNOW CALLUM'S YOUR FRIEND. DO YOU UNDERSTAND THAT THE ONLY WAY YOU WILL HURT HIM TODAY IS IF YOU DON'T TELL THE TRUTH?

YES, I KNOW THAT.

GOOD. SO I'LL ASK YOU *AGAIN,*

WHY DID CALLUM WANT YOU TO LEAVE THE SHOPPING CENTRE SO URGENTLY?

I *TOLD* YOU. HE WANTED TO SHOW ME SOMETHING OUTSIDE.

I *SEE.* TELL ME, MISS HADLEY. HOW WOULD YOU DESCRIBE CALLUM MCGREGOR?

OBJECTION, YOUR HONOUR!

WHAT HAS MISS HADLEY'S OPINION OF HER FRIEND HAVE TO DO WITH MY CLIENT?

I WAS WONDERING THAT MYSELF, MS ADAMS. OBJECTION SUSTAINED.

WHAT IS YOUR *RELATIONSHIP* WITH CALLUM MCGREGOR?

WE'RE FRIENDS. GOOD FRIENDS.

PERHAPS, *MORE* THAN... GOOD FRIENDS?

YOUR *HONOUR*...

I WITHDRAW MY QUESTION.

MISS HADLEY, DO YOU KNOW WHO IS RESPONSIBLE FOR THE BOMBING OF THE DUNDALE SHOPPING CENTRE.

OF *COURSE* NOT. HOW COULD I?

HOW *INDEED?* NO FURTHER QUESTIONS.

'CALL THE NEXT WITNESS.'

YOUR NAME IS LEO STOLL, CORRECT?

YES.

MR STOLL, COULD YOU TELL THE COURT WHAT YOU DO FOR A LIVING?

I'M A POLICE OFFICER – NOW RETIRED.

YOU DON'T LOOK OLD ENOUGH.

I WAS KNOCKED OVER BY A NOUGHT JOYRIDER. MY HIP WAS SMASHED.

I WAS OFFERED A DESK JOB BUT AFTER YEARS OUT IN THE FIELD, WELL, I COULDN'T FACE IT SO TOOK EARLY RETIREMENT.

DO YOU RECOGNISE THE DEFENDANT, RYAN MCGREGOR?

NEVER SEEN HIM BEFORE IN MY LIFE.

MR STOLL, HAVE YOU EVER SEEN CALLUM MCGREGOR BEFORE?

WHO?

CALLUM MCGREGOR, COULD YOU STAND UP PLEASE?

OH YES, I'VE SEEN *HIM* BEFORE. ON THAT AFTERNOON.

HE CAME INTO THE CAFÉ AND STARTED DRAGGING OUT A GIRL WHO'D BEEN MINDING HER OWN BUSINESS.

I ASKED IF SHE WAS OK. I MIGHT HAVE A DODGY HIP BUT I STILL KNOW A MOVE OR TWO.

AND WHAT HAPPENED THEN?

THE GIRL SAID HE WAS A FRIEND OF HERS AND HE WAS JUST TAKING HER OUT TO SHOW HER SOMETHING.

YOU'RE *SURE* THAT'S WHAT SHE SAID?

POSITIVE.

LIKE I SAID, I USED TO BE A POLICE OFFICER, SO I'VE BEEN TRAINED TO OBSERVE AND REMEMBER.

DID THE GIRL SEEM *SCARED* AT ALL?

NOT AT ALL. SHE WAS TREATING THE WHOLE THING LIKE IT WAS A BIG *JOKE.*

AND HOW COME YOU SURVIVED THE BOMB BLAST?

I FINISHED MY COFFEE AND LEFT LESS THAN A MINUTE AFTER THE BOY AND HIS FRIEND.

THANK YOU, MR STOLL. NO MORE QUESTIONS.

YOU DON'T KNOW EVERY DAMN THING!

YOU THINK YOU'RE THE *ONLY* ONE *HURTING* HERE.

RYAN MCGREGOR WAS MY FRIEND. SO WAS MEGGIE. D'YOU THINK I WANTED TO SEE HIM *HANG?*

WHY GO THEN?

BECAUSE... ONE DAY YOU'LL REALIZE YOU CAN'T ALWAYS DO WHAT YOU *WANT* IN THIS LIFE.

I TRIED TO *HELP.*

HOW? BY GETTING BLIND *DRUNK!*

YOU *STUPID* GIRL! WHO D'YOU THINK PAID FOR THEIR LAWYER AND LEGAL FEES!

I PRAYED AND ~~P~~AID AND DID EVERYTHING I ~~C~~OULD TO MAKE SURE RYAN WOULDN'T HANG.

AND THAT'S NOT TO LEAVE THIS ROOM, *UNDERSTAND?*

THAT'S YOUR GUILTY CONSCIENCE TALKING. YOU'VE NEVER DONE *ANYTHING* FOR ANYONE OTHER THAN *YOURSELF* IN YOUR LIFE.

GO BACK TO YOUR WINE BOTTLE. YOU'VE *EARNED* IT.

'IT'S OVER. THEY DIDN'T KILL ME QUICKLY. THEY DECIDED TO DRAW IT OUT INSTEAD.'

I'LL NEVER SEE THE OUTSIDE OF THIS PRISON AND WE ALL KNOW IT.

YOU MAY BUT *I'M* CERTAINLY NOT DONE YET. I'M CALLING IN EVERY FAVOUR I'M OWED — AND THEN SOME.

WITH ALL DUE RESPECT, MISS ADAMS, THIS IS AS FAR AS I WANT YOU TO GO.

RYAN, *PLEASE* DON'T GIVE UP. THERE'S STILL HOPE. WE CAN APPEAL.

I DON'T WANT YOU TO DO ANYTHING. IT'S OK LOVE, I'VE GOT IT ALL FIGURED.

RYAN, YOU'RE NOT GOING TO DO ANYTHING STUPID ARE YOU? *PROMISE* ME...

I'M AFRAID VISITING TIME IS OVER.

RYAN, PLEASE, *PLEASE* TRUST ME TO DO MY JOB. I WILL GET YOU OUT OF HERE. YOU HAVE TO BELIEVE IT.

RYAN...

DON'T YOU WORRY ABOUT ME. I'M GETTING OUT OF HERE MY WAY. YOU SEE IF I DON'T.

HE...HE DIDN'T EVEN SAY GOODBYE.

Later.

CALLUM! WHAT'RE YOU DOING?

TRYING NOT TO BE SEEN!

DID YOU PHONE ME? I DIDN'T HEAR YOUR SIGNAL.

NO, I CAME STRAIGHT HERE. I HID IN THE ROSE GARDEN 'TIL THE COAST WAS CLEAR.

Mother's agreed to my going to Chivers Boarding School.
I'm leaving at two o'clock on Sunday afternoon.
If I don't hear from you by then I'll know what your answer is.

I'll wait right up until the moment
I have to leave, but either way I'm going.
Take me away from this Callum.
   I want to be with you.
Please don't let me down.

I'll wait right up, but either
I have to leave, but either way
Take me away from this C
   I want to be with you.
Please don't let me down.

All my love.
Yours forever,
Sephy x

SARAH...

MISS SEPHY?

I...COULD YOU DO ME A FAVOUR?

COULD YOU DELIVER THIS LETTER TO CALLUM MCGREGOR? HE'S STAYING WITH HIS AUNT. THE ADDRESS IS ON THE FRONT.

I DON'T THINK SO. I *NEED* THIS JOB.

The next day.

CALLUM, YOUR CALL.

LEAVE IT TO ME, I'LL SORT IT OUT.

SOMETHING OF HERS, SOMETHING BLOODSTAINED SO IT CAN BE TESTED.

HOLD THIS AND READ FROM IT.

NO. I'M NOT GOING TO HELP YOU!

HOLD IT OR WE'LL BREAK YOUR ARMS AND HANG IT AROUND YOUR NECK.

I CAN DO THIS. I DON'T NEED YOU STANDING OVER ME, SUPERVISING.

NOT SUPERVISING. JUST OBSERVING, LITTLE BROTHER.

SHE'S ALL YOURS.

CALLUM, I... I UNDERSTAND WHY YOU HAVE TO DO THIS BUT IT'S **NOT** THE WAY.

AT CHIVERS, I BECAME INVOLVED WITH PROTESTS, DEBATES AND SIT-INS.

TRYING TO CHANGE THE WORLD USING VIOLENCE, YOU'LL JUST SWAP *ONE* FORM OF INJUSTICE FOR ANOTHER.

THERE ARE *OTHER* WAYS...

LIKE *WHAT?* LIKE BEING EDUCATED TO FIGHT THE SYSTEM FROM WITHIN. I *TRIED* THAT, REMEMBER?

WELL, I DON'T *WANT* YOUR HELP! YOUR CHARITY AND HANDOUTS!

YOU THINK WE NOUGHTS CAN'T DO *ANYTHING* WITH YOU LOT THERE TO *SUPERVISE!*

READ IT.

CALLUM...

READ IT.

CALLUM. WHEN...WHEN YOU DECIDE YOU DON'T *NEED* ME ANY MORE, I WANT YOU TO DO IT.

ONE LAST FAVOUR. IT'S THE LAST THING I'LL EVER ASK YOU. J-JUST MAKE IT *QUICK*, OK?

'ALL DONE? SHE DO THE BUSINESS?'

YEAH...

GIVE ME THE MEMORY CARD.

WELL DONE LITTLE BROTHER.

PETE AND I WILL DELIVER THIS ALONG WITH OUR DEMANDS. WE'LL BE BACK BY MORNING.

IF THE GENERAL'S SECOND-IN-COMMAND SHOWS UP FIRST, MAKE HIM WELCOME – THE PASSWORD'S *GOLDEN MAN*.

Later.

YOU LOOK AS IF YOU COULD USE SOME COMPANY.

LEILA? WHO'S GUARDING THE FRONT?

I CAME FOR A LOO BREAK.

YOU *CAN'T* JUST LEAVE YOUR POST LIKE THAT! YOU CAN'T LEAVE US *UNGUARDED!*

YOU DON'T HAVE TO GET DRESSED ON MY ACCOUNT.

YES, I *DO.* YOU'RE BEING BLOODY *STUPID!* GO, GUARD THE FRONT LIKE YOU'RE SUPPOSED TO!

FINE! YOU'RE MAD AS HELL ABOUT SOMETHING, BUT DON'T TAKE IT OUT ON ME!

'I'M HERE TO SEE YOUR PRISONER.'

I HOPE FOR YOUR SAKE, YOUR FATHER LOVES YOU VERY, VERY MUCH.

BE A GOOD GIRL AND YOU'LL BE OUT OF HERE SOON.

MAKE SURE SHE DOESN'T LEAVE THAT ROOM ALIVE.

ORDERS FROM THE GENERAL HIMSELF. UNDERSTOOD?

YES, SIR. I'LL TAKE CARE OF IT MYSELF.

GOOD MAN. MAKE SURE YOU DO.

Later.

SEPHY? SEPHY, WHAT'S THE MATTER?

IT'S NOTHING. GO AWAY.

YOU'RE HURTING?

LIKE *YOU* CARE!

THIS IS FROM BACK ON THE BEACH, WHEN LEILA HIT YOU. I'M SORRY.

THEN LET ME GO, *PLEASE.*

I...I CAN'T.

SEPHY, I LOVE YOU.

NO, YOU *DON'T.* LOVE DOESN'T EXIST BETWEEN NOUGHTS AND CROSSES. YOU TOLD ME SO.

YOU'RE SURE?

POSITIVE. AND HE WORE THE SAME BOOTS, THE ONES WITH THE SILVER CHAINS.

THANKS. NOW *GO*, HURRY.

'I WILL MAKE A SHORT STATEMENT AND THAT'S ALL. DOCTORS DESCRIBE MY DAUGHTER'S CONDITION AS CRITICAL BUT STABLE. SHE'S EXHAUSTED. SHE'S BEEN THROUGH A *GREAT DEAL* AND TRAVELLED FAR TO GET HOME TO US.'

THE POLICE ARE PRESENT AND WILL INTERVIEW HER WHEN SHE REGAINS CONSCIOUSNESS.

ACTING ON INFORMATION RECEIVED, WE CAPTURED ONE OF THE KIDNAPPERS AND ANOTHER OPENED FIRE ON THE POLICE AND WAS KILLED AS A RESULT.

NO RANSOM HAS BEEN PAID. THAT'S ALL I'D LIKE TO SAY AT THIS TIME. THANK YOU.

SHE'S *LYING!* THERE'S NO *WAY* ANDREW DORN'S A TRAITOR.

HE'S THE GENERAL'S SECOND-IN-COMMAND FOR GOD'S SAKE!

SHE MADE IT UP, T'MAKE US PARANOID ABOUT EACH OTHER, THAT'S WHAT!

SO, HOW DID THE POLICE KNOW WHERE YOU'D BE? ONLY *FIVE* PEOPLE KNEW OUR PLANS APART FROM DORN. ONE'S CAPTURED AND ONE'S *DEAD.*

YOU CHANGED YOUR POSITIONS AT THE LAST MINUTE AND DIDN'T HAVE CHANCE TO TELL HIM, THAT'S WHAT SAVED YOU.

HE ORDERED ME TO KILL SEPHY REGARDLESS OF WHAT HAPPENED. I THINK THAT'S BECAUSE HE KNEW SHE'D RECOGNIZED HIM.

SEPHY WAS *RIGHT.* HE *BETRAYED* US.

I'LL *KILL* HIM IF IT'S THE *LAST* THING I DO!

NO, WE'LL *EXPOSE* HIM. EXCEPT WE DON'T HAVE ANY PROOF. NONE OF US HAS THE EAR OF THE GENERAL.

ANY MESSAGE TO HIM HAS TO GO THROUGH DORN AND HE *CAN'T* SUSPECT WE'RE ONTO HIM.

WE'LL HAVE TO BIDE OUR TIME. IT'S BEST IF WE SPLIT UP FOR A WHILE. TOGETHER WE'LL BE EASIER TO TRACK DOWN.

MEANTIME MORE OF OUR PEOPLE GO TO *JAIL* OR *HANG?*

WHAT? NO, IT...IT'S A TUMMY BUG.

THAT'S LASTED A COUPLE OF MONTHS?

YOU'VE BEEN CALLING ON THE PORCELAIN TELEPHONE EVERY MORNING FOR WEEKS NOW.

I DON'T KNOW WHAT YOU'RE TALKING ABOUT!

WHAT ABOUT THE BAGGY T-SHIRTS AND JUMPERS YOU'VE STARTED WEARING? TO CONCEAL THE FACT THE BUMP'S STARTING TO SHOW!

I'M ONLY WEARING THEM BECAUSE...BECAUSE... OH, MINNIE!

OH, SEPHY, YOU IDIOT! YOU COULD HAVE TOLD ME. I COULD HAVE HELPED YOU. WE ALL COULD.

MINNIE, I DON'T KNOW WHAT TO DO.

YOU'RE GOING TO HAVE TO TELL MOTHER.

ARE YOU INSANE?

SHE'LL FIND OUT SOONER OR LATER. EVEN IF YOU MANAGED TO HIDE YOUR ENTIRE PREGNANCY, HOW D'YOU EXPECT TO HIDE A BABY?

WOULD YOU DO WITH ALL THE MONEY IN THE WORLD?

I DON'T LIKE TO DWELL ON WHAT I'LL NEVER HAVE.

DON'T YOU HAVE ANY DREAMS OR ARE YOU TOO GOOD TO SHARE THEM WITH US?

I'D BUILD A ROCKET, LEAVE THIS PLANET AND LIVE ON THE MOON. ANYPLACE ELSE BUT HERE.

WHY? IF YOU HAD ALL THAT MONEY YOU COULD DO WHATEVER YOU LIKED RIGHT HERE!

DREAM ON! YOU KNOW WHAT THEY CALL A NOUGHT WITH ALL THE MONEY IN THE WORLD? A BLANKER.

NAH, THINGS WOULD CHANGE IF YOU WERE LOADED.

IT TAKES MORE THAN THAT. IT TAKES DETERMINATION AND SACRIFICE AND ...AND.

AH, FORGET IT. IGNORE ME.

WE'LL HAVE TO CALL YOU THE DEEP ONE. BETTER YET, THE PROFOUND ONE!

WE'LL COME TO YOU FOR SPIRITUAL GUIDANCE. OH, PROFOUND ONE, SHARE YOUR MYSTICAL INSIGHTS WITH US...

OY! IF YOU THREE CAN'T BE BOTHERED TO GET ON WITH YOUR WORK, THERE'S *HUNDREDS* WHO'D BE HAPPY TO HAVE YOUR JOBS!

WHAT A HORSE'S ASS!

THERE'S A LOT OF IT ABOUT.

AMEN TO *THAT.*

WHAT I WANT TO KNOW IS...

...HAS REFUSED TO CONFIRM OR DENY THAT PERSEPHONE MIRA HADLEY, HIS DAUGHTER, IS PREGNANT AS A RESULT OF HER ORDEAL A FEW MONTHS AGO.

SHUSH! SHUSH!

WE CAN ONLY SPECULATE AS TO HER TREATMENT AT THE HAND OF THE NOUGHT MEN WHO ABDUCTED HER.

PERSEPHONE HAS SO FAR REFUSED TO SPEAK OF HER ORDEAL, THE MEMORIES BEING OBVIOUSLY TOO PAINFUL, TOO SHOCKING...

I'M LEAVING.

OH NO YOU *DON'T!*

WATCH ME!

Later.

OH, SEPHY... SEPHY...

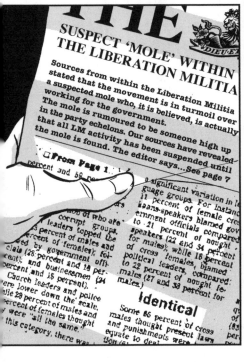

WELL DONE, JUDE.

WHY?

MY DAUGHTER WON'T BE ABLE TO PUT THIS WHOLE BUSINESS BEHIND HER AND GET ON WITH HER LIFE IF YOU DON'T.

SHE FEELS SHE *OWES* YOU SOMETHING FOR SAVING HER LIFE.

IF SHE KNEW YOU WEREN'T GOING TO DIE, THEN SHE'D BE ONLY TOO WILLING TO GET RID OF YOUR CHILD.

A CHILD SHE NEVER WANTED. A CHILD SHE STILL *DOESN'T*.

AND SHE TOLD YOU THIS, DID SHE?

OF COURSE.

IS IT JUST THE THOUGHT OF SEPHY AND I HAVING A CHILD *TOGETHER* THAT YOU CAN'T STAND, OR IS IT *ALL* MIXED RACE CHILDREN IN GENERAL?

WE'RE NOT HERE TO DISCUSS MY FEELINGS.

WHAT'S YOUR ANSWER?

I NEED TO THINK ABOUT IT.

I WANT YOUR ANSWER HERE AND *NOW*.

WELL?

YOUR GIRL, PERSEPHONE HADLEY TRIED TO GET IN HERE TO SEE YOU — MORE THAN ONCE.

BUT ORDERS CAME FROM *WAY* ABOVE THE GOVERNOR'S HEAD THAT SAID YOU WERE TO HAVE NO VISITORS WHATSOEVER.

JACK, YOU'VE BEEN FAIR AND DECENT TO ME, MORE THAN I THOUGHT ANY NOUGHT COULD BE AND I APPRECIATE THAT.

I NEED TO ASK YOU A FAVOUR... IT MIGHT GET YOU INTO TROUBLE.

MY DULL LIFE COULD DO WITH A BIT OF SPRUCING UP.

COULD YOU FIND A WAY TO GET THIS LETTER TO SEPHY?

SURE THING.

YOU'LL PUT IT *PERSONALLY* INTO HER HAND. *PROMISE?*

I PROMISE.

CALLUM, IT'S TIME.

BIRTH ANNOUNCEMENTS

At midnight on 14th May at Mercy Community Hospital, to Persephone Hadley and Callum McGregor (deceased) a beautiful daughter, Callie Rose.

Persephone wishes it to be known that her daughter Callie Rose will be taking her father's name of McGregor.